BIONICLE®

METRU NUI · CITY OF LEGENDS

TOA VAKAMA · TOA WHENUA · TOA ONEWA
TOA MATAU · TOA NOKAMA · TOA NUJU

SCHOLASTIC INC.

New York · Toronto · London · Auckland · Sydney
Mexico City · New Delhi · Hong Kong · Buenos Aires

W9-AXZ-880

T 17931

ISBN 0-439-60734-5

12 11 10 9 8 7 6 5 4 3 2 1   4 5 6 7 8/0

Printed in the U.S.A.

First printing, August 2004

INTRODUCTION

In the time before time, there existed a vast, beautiful city called Metru Nui. Here thousands of Matoran worked, played, and lived their lives, under the watchful eye of their leader, Turaga Dume.

The Matoran believed they would always be safe and secure in their home. But a time of darkness, betrayal, and danger was fast approaching. A time that would threaten the very existence of Metru Nui and its citizens. To combat it, six Toa Metru would risk their lives against powerful enemies and forces far beyond anything they could imagine.

This book is a guide to this amazing City of Legends, from the towering Coliseum to the protodermis canals to the depths of the Ta-Metru fire pits. In this book, you will tour the six districts, or metru, and meet the heroic Toa, cold and efficient Vahki enforcers, strange and powerful Dark Hunters, and bizarre Rahi who live there.

The mysteries of Metru Nui are waiting for you.

GA-METRU

Known for its peace and tranquility, Ga-Metru is the spiritual and educational center of Metru Nui. Temples and schools line the beautiful protodermis canals that run through the district. Ga-Matoran so love the atmosphere here that they rarely leave the metru unless they have to, and then their travels normally take them to the relative quiet of the Onu-Metru Archives.

No Matoran who travels the streets of Ga-Matru or stands on the shore of the silver sea of protodermis ever forgets the experience. Some would even say that you can almost hear the voices of the Great Beings here. Legend has it that this was the second metru constructed after Ta-Metru and the one most favored by Mata Nui, the spiritual guardian of the city.

THE GREAT TEMPLE

Many Matoran would say that this is the most important building in all of Metru Nui, rivaled only by the Coliseum. Built on a spit of land so that it stands apart from the rest of the metru, the Great Temple is a haven for those who are troubled and a symbol of hope for all citizens.

Deep within the Great Temple lies the Toa suva, a round stone structure said to be the source of Toa powers. The suva has six slots designed to hold the mysterious artifacts known as Toa stones. After placing the stones inside those slots, six Matoran were transformed into the mighty Toa Metru.

Once activated, the sides of the suva fell away, revealing a collection of Toa tools. Also inside the suva were six disks bearing the images of the Toa Metru's masks. The Toa believe this was a sign that they were always destined to become heroes.

The Great Temple is heavily guarded by the city's order enforcement squads, known as Vahki. Though they will normally allow Matoran to come and go from the site, they will respond swiftly to any signs of disorder here.

PROTODERMIS

The city of Metru Nui rests on a sea of silver liquid known as protodermis. With no fresh- or saltwater anywhere in the city, this is what the Matoran view as the "stuff of life." It is the source of almost everything constructed in the city.

Protodermis comes in three known types:

Liquid protodermis, such as that in the sea, which must be purified before it can be used for creation.

Solid protodermis, mined in Onu-Metru and used for works of art and building materials. Every building in the city is made of solid protodermis.

Energized protodermis, the rarest form. Its origins remain a mystery. Onu-Metru miners have stumbled upon small amounts of this substance, which seems to have the ability to cause radical changes in life-forms immersed in it. Although samples of this have been provided to Ga-Metru schools for study, no one has ever succeeded in discovering its properties or duplicating it. Like raw liquid protodermis, energized protodermis is silver in color.

Liquid protodermis is drawn into Ga-Metru from the sea via a channel, which passes into the Great Temple. Here all purification work is done by a special group of Ga-Matoran. While a few read passages in an ancient Matoran dialect asking for the protection and aid of Mata Nui, the others supervise the rapid heating and cooling of the liquid to remove impurities. When the process is finished, the protodermis has turned clear and taken on a bluish color.

From the Great Temple, protodermis travels in different directions. Some is directed over the falls in Ga-Metru and into the canals, which wind through other parts of the city and dump their contents into a subterranean pipe system. Other protodermis is passed through pipes and superheated on its way to the foundries of Ta-Metru, to be used in the creation of masks, tools, and other items. Molten protodermis that goes unused is allowed to return to the sea.

GA–METRU

THE SCHOOLS

Ga-Metru is evenly divided between teachers and students. In fact, the pursuit of learning is so valued there that the metru employs Matoran from other districts to take care of many jobs. This frees the Ga-Matoran to focus on their roles as teachers or students.

Ga-Metru schools teach the history of Metru Nui, ancient Matoran dialects, and the science of protodermis, among other things. Students spend time in classrooms and labs, but they also take trips to see interesting carvings or new exhibits in the Archives. The very best students get to work in the Great Temple as protodermis purifiers.

TOA NOKAMA

Element: Water

Tools: Twin hydroblades

Mask: Kanohi Rau, Great Mask of Translation. Allows the user to translate and communicate in any written or spoken language.

Nokama was a well-respected teacher in Ga-Metru before she became a Toa. She is smart and resourceful but sometimes talks when she should listen. She considers Vakama to be her best friend among the Toa Metru, although she does enjoy joking around with Matau. Nokama takes being a Toa very seriously. But sometimes she misses her old life and her Matoran friends. She is sure she can be a good Toa, but she is not certain she will ever get used to the demands of being a heroine.

VHISOLA

Vhisola is a student in Ga-Metru and always thought of Nokama as her best friend. She even kept all sorts of items related to Nokama in her house. But she would get very jealous if Nokama spent time with any other friends, and it only got worse when Nokama became a Toa Metru. Vhisola knew a secret — the location of one of the six legendary Great Kanoka Disks, artifacts of great power. She decided to use that knowledge to make herself more famous than Nokama. When knowing the secret put her life in danger, she changed her mind and helped Nokama obtain the Great Disk.

BORDAKH

Metru Nui is patrolled by Vahki order enforcement squads, mechanical beings programmed to preserve order at any cost. Vahki are equipped with Kanoka disks and special stun staffs. Operating from central task force hives in each metru, the Vahki insure that Rahi rampages are contained and Matoran do not wander away from their jobs. The Vahki are always around to look after the Matoran, whether they like it or not.

The Ga-Metru order enforcement squad is made up of Bordakh, among the most cunning of all Vahki. Bordakh work in small, highly mobile squads, and it's said they love the chase more than anything. Their Staffs of Loyalty make a Matoran so enthusiastic about the ideas of order and security that she will actively look for "troublemakers" to turn in to the Vahki.

CREATURES OF GA-METRU

The Dweller in the Deep

Long thought to be a myth by Ga-Matoran, this creature was said to live at the very bottom of the sea. It was believed to be the only natural enemy of the dreaded Tarakava serpents. Nokama learned that these legends were not just empty tales. On the day she dove deep to retrieve the Great Disk, she found the Great Disk inside the jaws of an incredible beast that pursued her to the surface. Witnesses saw only a massive, sleek shape and jaws that seemed wide enough to swallow the Great Temple whole. It has since returned to its home beneath the waves.

Kavinika

When these wolflike creatures were branded a pest in Po-Metru, Ga-Matoran adopted them for use as guard Rahi at lesser temples and protodermis labs. But the kavinika proved so short-tempered and ferocious that the experiment was deemed a failure. The Ga-Matoran tried to drive the kavinika out, but some still roam around the outskirts of the metru.

PO-METRU

Walking into Po-Metru is like entering another world. Instead of the tall buildings that mark Ko-Metru and Ta-Metru, you see a ridge of mountains. Roads are replaced by well-worn pathways of dirt and stone. Rather than spending their work time indoors, most Po-Matoran labor all day in the light of the suns. Only the presence of chutes and the sight of airships in the sky serve as reminders that you are still in Metru Nui.

This is the home of the carvers. Here items made in Ta-Metru are engraved and decorated, larger creations are assembled, and great statues are chiseled from blocks of solid protodermis. Po-Matoran are the most talented craftworkers in all the city.

PO-METRU

FIELDS OF CONSTRUCTION

This large, open area is where assorted pieces are assembled into items that can be used all over Metru Nui. Everything from furniture to telescreens to Vahki are built here. The sole exception is transport vehicles, which are manufactured in Le-Metru.

BUILDING A VAHKI

Although the original design for the Vahki came from an Onu-Matoran, Nuparu, and the parts were forged in Ta-Metru, it is the Po-Matoran who bring these mechanical beings to life. Two separate assembly areas exist for Vahki, one to fit the larger parts together and one to install the clockwork mechanisms into the skull casing. When the work is completed, another coldly efficient order enforcement mechanoid is ready for duty. Being purely mechanical, Vahki cannot be "killed," only broken.

Vahki are created with very simple behavior patterns installed. Their job is to maintain order, whether that means stopping Rahi from rampaging through the city or making sure Matoran stay on the job during their work shift. Although Vahki are capable of understanding

Matoran speech, they communicate only through ultrasonic signals. Turaga Dume's chamber in the Coliseum is fitted with technology that translates these signals into speech.

There is an old joke in Metru Nui, "Don't look back, a Vahki might be gaining on you." These enforcers live for the chase. They cannot be argued with or reasoned with. A Matoran lawbreaker has only two choices, surrender or run. Choosing to surrender will result in the Vahki using their stun staffs to either make the Matoran more willing to work or less able to cause disorder. Fleeing will delay the inevitable for a while, but eventually the Vahki will track down their prey.

Vahki are capable of three different modes of transport. They can walk on two legs; walk on four, using their staffs as forelegs; or shift into a more aerodynamic mode for flight.

Most Vahki are not good swimmers, with the Bordakh being the only ones designed to withstand time underwater (and even they avoid it).

In addition to the six models of Vahki active in the city, the Po-Matoran have constructed two special types of order enforcer:

KRAAHU

The Kraahu has one major advantage over the standard Vahki model. Unlike the Vahki, which have a centralized intelligence mechanism, a Kraahu's clockwork knowledge centers are scattered throughout its body. This allows the Kraahu to split apart and its various pieces to function independently. When intact, the Kraahu can emit clouds of stun gas. Split apart, each Kraahu piece carries an electrical charge that is triggered on contact. Kraahu are normally dispatched to deal with large numbers of Rahi on the loose.

KRANUA

Powerful and bulky, the Kranua is capable of transforming its body into animated grains of protodermis. In this form, it can flow through narrow cracks or vanish into the pavement before re-forming someplace else. This talent makes the Kranua particularly difficult to escape from or trap.

ASSEMBLER'S VILLAGE

Settlements like this can be found all over Po-Metru. Here Matoran live in small shacks and work at outdoor stations, putting pieces together and doing intricate carving. Due to the fact that these villages are scattered among the mountains and canyons, they can be very dangerous places to live. There are far too many of them for the Vahki to guard effectively, so Rahi can strike and escape long before help can arrive. Po-Matoran spend a great deal of time practicing their Kanoka disk launching so they can better defend themselves.

THE SCULPTURE FIELDS

These great, barren plains are dotted with huge statues created by Po-Matoran carvers. The sculptures are so large that very few enclosed buildings in the city could house them, so they must be created and displayed outdoors. Once finished, the statues are transported by fleets of airships to various parts of the city.

Portions of the Sculpture Fields have become unstable due to repeated Rahi activity. As a result, some of the statues have begun to sink into the soft ground. Certain areas are now completely closed to Matoran and the statues residing there are considered lost for good.

The Po-Metru Great Disk was found embedded in a rock pillar in the Sculpture Fields.

PO-METRU

DON'T MISS ...

Hewkii's Disks

Hewkii is the most skilled disk maker in all of Po-Metru, and his Kanoka are considered the best for use in sport. Matoran from other metru have been known to come to Po-Metru to trade for Hewkii's disks. This forced Turaga Dume to create a rule that players from other metru cannot use Po-Metru disks in citywide tournaments.

CANYON OF UNENDING WHISPERS

This once lonely spot on the border of Po-Metru and Onu-Metru has become the scene of a great deal of activity in recent times. Large numbers of Vahki Zadakh have been seen moving in and out of the canyon. Some Matoran have also mentioned seeing a strange four-legged creature and a massive brute slipping down the trails that lead to the caverns. The reasons for all this sudden activity in a desolate region of the metru remain a mystery.

TOA ONEWA

Element: Stone

Tools: Proto pitons

Toa Onewa is strong-willed, sharp, and stubborn. A former carver, he is most comfortable with things he can see and touch, so he has little patience for Vakama's visions. Onewa prefers doing to talking and thinks the Toa spend too much time planning and debating. He is extremely daring and refuses to even consider the possibility of defeat.

Onewa has not made made any close friends among the other Toa, but that does not seem to bother him. He particularly likes to needle Nuju and Whenua, since he thinks worrying about the past or the future is a waste of time.

AHKMOU

Ahkmou is a builder and carver, very skilled at a number of things but not a master of any. He has come in second to Onewa in everything his whole life, and this led to bitterness and resentment. His discovery of the location of the Po-Metru Great Disk brought him to the attention of two villainous Dark Hunters. They persuaded him to lure five other Matoran into traps and to try to get the other five Great Disks. Ahkmou's plan failed due to the intervention of the Toa Metru. He disappeared shortly after the defeat of the Morbuzakh.

ZADAKH

Vahki Zadakh are huge, strong, very fast, and fearless, some might even say reckless. They are always the first ones into a fight and the last ones left standing. Zadakh Staffs of Suggestion leave a Matoran susceptible to influence for the duration of the charge, usually several hours.

CREATURES OF PO-METRU

Kikanalo

Massive creatures resembling a cross between a kangaroo and an elephant, great herds of Kikanalo sweep across the plains and canyons of Po-Metru every day. Using their sharp tusks, they churn up the rocky ground, dislodging bits of protodermis that have been lost during the carvers' labors. These scraps can later be collected by Po-Matoran and recycled for later use. The valuable service the Kikanalo provide explains why the Matoran ignore how often the beasts trample entire villages in their wild stampedes.

Tunnelers

These creatures resemble great lizards. As their name suggests, they live underground and use their claws to tunnel through solid stone. The tunneler defends itself by changing its body mass to match any material it comes into contact with. For example, a tunneler struck by a fireball will become a creature of fire. The only way to defeat a tunneler is to somehow bring it into contact with a substance that will leave it with a weaker form, such as glass or water.

KO-METRU

Matoran call Ko-Metru "the quiet metru." It combines the utter silence of some parts of Ga-Metru with the barren feeling of Po-Metru to create an atmosphere that keeps even visiting Le-Matoran's mouths shut. All traveling in Ko-Metru is done in the shadow of the massive, crystalline Knowledge Towers that line the streets.

Ko-Matoran have a reputation for being as cold and hard as those towers. The truth is that they are simply dedicated to a goal. Virtually every Ko-Matoran hopes one day to work in a Knowledge Tower, so their time is spent studying and learning as much as they can. They have little patience for anyone or anything that distracts them from their studies.

KO-METRU

Ko-Metru is the only district that actively feuds with another. Ko-Matoran and Onu-Matoran have been arguing for years over which is more important: studying the past or trying to predict the future. It's gotten so bad that Ko-Matoran have gone to Turaga Dume to argue against expansion of the Archives, and Onu-Matoran have now and then "accidentally" undermined Knowledge Towers, resulting in the need for lengthy repairs.

THE KNOWLEDGE TOWERS

The towers of Ko-Metru reach so high into the sky that their roofs are capped with snow and ice. Inside, hundreds of scholars study prophecies, make predictions, and watch the stars looking for signs of things to come.

Knowledge Towers are some of the most unusual structures in Metru Nui, because they are not built, they are grown. Knowledge crystals about the size of a Matoran's hand are thrown into special cradles located at different places in the district. From there, they grow at a rapid pace until a new tower stands alongside the old ones.

Each Knowledge Tower features extensive library space, living quarters for scholars, observatories to monitor the stars, and special areas where valuable tablets and carvings that detail ancient prophecies are kept. It's said that once they enter the Knowledge Towers, some Ko-Matoran spend their entire lives there, never setting foot outside.

TOWERS OF THOUGHT

This special class of Knowledge Tower is intended for the most important research projects in Ko-Metru. Absolute silence is required of all who enter these structures. A Vahki squad is always on patrol nearby to apprehend anyone who disturbs the work of the Ko-Matoran in these towers.

KANOKA DISKS

One of the major discoveries to come out of the Knowledge Towers was the means to create disks from liquid protodermis. Working together with

protodermis labs in Ga-Metru, scholars perfected the process, and the Kanoka disk rapidly became a part of daily life in Metru Nui.

Kanoka are round disks of protodermis, each with a special power. Each disk is stamped with a symbol of the metru in which it was made, and a three-digit code. The first digit relates to the metru in which the disk was made, the second its power, and the third to the power level.

Kanoka disks have many uses:

Sport: Disks are used in all sorts of games in Metru Nui, including disk surfing, chute boarding, and other sports.

Defense: Matoran use the disks to fight off Rahi beasts and other threats.

Mask Making: Kanohi Masks of Power are made from Kanoka disks. Kanoka with power levels 1 to 6 are made into Matoran masks, because the power leeches away during the mask-making process. Power level 7 disks are made into Noble Masks of Power. Power level 8 disks are made into Great Masks of Power like the Toa wear. Only six power level 9 disks are known to exist. They are the Great Disks that the Toa recovered from hiding places all over the city.

Kanoka disks are made by pouring purified liquid protodermis into special molds. Often this process is repeated several times before the disk is pronounced done. The nature and level of the disk's power is determined by the properties of the protodermis used, its purity, and the skill of the Matoran making it. Even after all this time, Matoran are still unable to predict just how powerful a disk will be or what power it will have.

The metru in which it is made determines the flight characteristics of the disk (see the chart on page 30). There are also eight basic Kanoka disk powers:

DON'T MISS...

Matoro's Rahi

Of all the Ko-Matoran, only Matoro enjoys a good relationship with the Onu-Matoran. He spends much of his time in the Archives, studying different Rahi, trying to master their languages and behavior patterns. Now and then he comes upon small creatures that the Archives are not interested in, and these he trades to other Matoran who are seeking pets.

Reconstitutes at random: Temporarily scrambles the molecules of the target, resulting in a new shape.

Freezes: Covers the target in a thick coating of ice.

Weakens: Reduces the strength of a living or nonliving target. Can be used to bring down structures.

Removes poison: Cures the effects of toxic substances.

Enlarges: Causes target to grow. Rate of growth is tied to the power level of the disk.

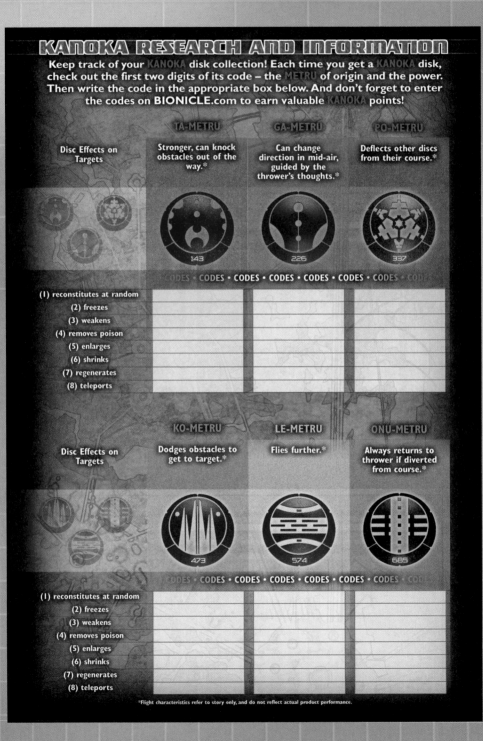

KANOKA RESEARCH AND INFORMATION

Keep track of your KANOKA disk collection! Each time you get a KANOKA disk, check out the first two digits of its code – the METRU of origin and the power. Then write the code in the appropriate box below. And don't forget to enter the codes on BIONICLE.com to earn valuable KANOKA points!

Disc Effects on Targets	TA-METRU Stronger, can knock obstacles out of the way.*	GA-METRU Can change direction in mid-air, guided by the thrower's thoughts.*	PO-METRU Deflects other discs from their course.*
	143	226	337

CODES • CODES • CODES • CODES • CODES • CODES • CODES • COD

(1) reconstitutes at random			
(2) freezes			
(3) weakens			
(4) removes poison			
(5) enlarges			
(6) shrinks			
(7) regenerates			
(8) teleports			

Disc Effects on Targets	KO-METRU Dodges obstacles to get to target.*	LE-METRU Flies further.*	ONU-METRU Always returns to thrower if diverted from course.*
	473	574	685

CODES • CODES • CODES • CODES • CODES • CODES • CODES • COD

(1) reconstitutes at random			
(2) freezes			
(3) weakens			
(4) removes poison			
(5) enlarges			
(6) shrinks			
(7) regenerates			
(8) teleports			

*Flight characteristics refer to story only, and do not reflect actual product performance.

Shrinks: Causes target to reduce in size. Rate of shrinkage is tied to the power level of the disk.

Regenerates: Can be used to repair a target, normally a structure or piece of equipment.

Teleports: Transports target to another location. Range of teleportation is tied to the power level of the disk.

During the disk-making process, multiple Kanoka can be combined to form disks with totally new powers. In some cases, disk makers know what the combinations will result in. Other times, it is a case of trial and error.

In addition to being launched and thrown, Kanoka disks are also built into many devices in Metru Nui. Disks of levitation and increase weight are incorporated into Le-Matoran airships, and disks of speed into some ground vehicles. Some newer buildings even have disks of regeneration built into them, so that with the tug of a chain any damage to the structure can be instantly repaired.

TOA NUJU

Element: Ice

Mask: Kanohi Matatu, the Great Mask of Telekinesis

Tools: Twin crystal spikes

To some, Toa Nuju seems unfriendly and cold, and in some ways that is a true picture of him. But at heart he simply is used to working alone and not having to deal with others, so being in a team is not a comfortable situation for him. He has made it clear that he is willing to accept Vakama as leader "as long as he doesn't expect me to follow." What he would really like is the chance to go back to his work in Ko-Metru and forget about saving entire cities.

Toa Nuju respects Nokama, can tolerate Vakama, and has managed to set aside at least a few of his differences with Whenua. Onewa and Matau get on his nerves and he would rather not work with them.

ISBN: S-TK9-60734-5

EHRYE

This Ko-Matoran had one great ambition: to be a scholar in a Knowledge Tower. But Nuju believed he was too reckless for the job, so Ehrye had to stick to running errands around the metru. When he discovered the location of a Great Disk, he thought he had found his ticket to success. Instead, he was almost trapped forever by a pair of Dark Hunters. Ehrye later told Nuju where to find the legendary disk. He is currently missing.

KO-METRU

KEERAKH

The Ko-Metru Vahki have taken the uncertainty out of pursuit. They are known for the uncanny ability to figure out where their target is going and to get there first. Keerakh Staffs of Confusion temporarily scramble a Matoran's sense of time and place, making them so disoriented that they can't cause any more trouble. It's not unusual to see confused Ko-Matoran wandering through the metru, not sure where they are or what they are doing there.

CREATURES OF KO-METRU

Ice Bats

These nasty flying creatures perch on the tops of the Knowledge Towers and have resisted all efforts by Ko-Matoran and Vahki to drive them away. While not particularly dangerous to Matoran, they do have a habit of flying into observatories and smashing valuable equipment as they try to find their way back out. They also pose a hazard to Matoran airships, which is why the vessels tend to avoid passing over Ko-Metru.

Kralhi

This mechanical creation was the prototype for the Vahki, the Metru Nui order enforcement squads. Based on an idea conceived in Ko-Metru, the Kralhi can launch an energy bubble from its tail to enclose a target. The Kralhi then drains energy from its captive into itself, leaving the lawbreaker too weak to cause trouble. Unfortunately, it also left the Matoran too weak to work, which made the Kralhi a not very efficient solution to the problem. They were "retired," but efforts to turn them off failed. About two dozen are still at large, a few in Ko-Metru and a few in little-used parts of the Archives. The whereabouts of the rest are unknown.

The Heroes of Metru Nui

TA-METRU

ross into Ta-Metru and the first thing you will notice is the heat. It comes in waves from hundreds of furnaces and foundries and rivers of molten protodermis, so intense it is almost suffocating to one who is not used to it. The skies are full of steam and smoke vented from the massive, cone-shaped factories. And everywhere, there is the clatter and banging of Ta-Matoran laborers hard at work.

It's no wonder that Matoran from other metru try to avoid visiting this place. At the same time, they know that Ta-Metru is the most important site in the city. It's the district where Masks of Power, tools, disk launchers, and virtually everything else used in Metru Nui are forged from molten protodermis. It's hard work, and a wise being knows not to interrupt a Ta-Matoran while he is doing it: a single, tiny flaw can ruin a day's work and send an item to the scrap heap to be melted down again.

THE MASK MAKERS

A small number of highly skilled Ta-Matoran earn the privilege of becoming mask makers. They are responsible for creating every Mask of Power in the city, from the ones worn by the Matoran to the Great Masks worn by Toa.

Kanoka disks are used to make masks. There are two methods used to make Kanohi masks:

A Matoran takes a disk, melts it down, and pours the molten protodermis into a mask mold. After it has cooled, it is removed from the mold and any flaws pounded out by the mask maker. A skilled crafter may spend many days at his forge trying to get a mask just right.

The mask maker combines two or more Kanoka disks into one. He then carves the Kanohi from the disk using a mask-making tool, which resembles a small torch. Combining Kanoka disks allows the mask maker to create new mask powers. For example, combining a Kanoka disk with the *growth* power and a disk with the *regenerate* power results in a Mask of Shielding.

Before he became a Toa Metru, Vakama was a skilled mask maker in Ta-Metru. He even did special jobs for Turaga Dume. His most recent request from the Turaga was to create a Mask of Time.

After a mask is done, it may go to any one of a number of places. If it is a Noble Mask or a Great Mask, it is sent to Ga-Metru and placed in the Great Temple. If it is a Matoran mask, it sent to Po-Metru for finishing and distribution. If the mask is flawed in some way, it is sent to the protodermis reclamation yard in Ta-Metru to be melted down.

All other goods made in Ta-Metru are shipped to Po-Metru, where carvers and other workers ready them for use.

THE GREAT FURNACE

In a metru full of factories and furnaces, one stood out above them all. The Great Furnace towered well over a thousand feet in the air, second only in height to the Coliseum. Its heat was so intense that even Ta-Matoran could not work there for more than a few minutes at a time.

A short time ago, workers in the Great Furnace were being attacked by massive vines that appeared from nowhere and disappeared again. Fearing for their safety, the workers fled. The Great Furnace eventually became the hiding place for the monstrous king root of the Morbuzakh plant. During the battle between the Toa Metru and the Morbuzakh, the Great Furnace was destroyed. It has yet to be rebuilt.

THE MORBUZAKH

This blackened, twisted plant threatened to turn all of Metru Nui into rubble. Its vines were powerful enough to crush entire buildings. Matoran did their best to defend their homes and workplaces against this menace that seemed to strike from everywhere at once. The lucky Matoran were able to run to safety. Others vanished completely.

The Morbuzakh vines first appeared on the outskirts of Ta-Metru. The vines quickly drove Matoran away from the area, forcing them to flee toward the heart of the city. The Toa Metru later discovered that the king root of the Morbuzakh was intelligent and intended to take over the city and turn the Matoran into its slaves.

Using the six Great Kanoka Disks, the Toa Metru were able to destroy the Morbuzakh. They never realized that someone had actually commanded the Morbuzakh to attack the city, but the identity of that being remains a mystery. Despite the disappearance of the vines throughout the city, most Matoran still refuse to return to outlying areas for fear that the Morbuzakh will return.

DON'T MISS ...

Takua's Trade Goods

Although not very skilled as a toolmaker, Takua loves to travel more than almost any other Matoran. He is always visiting other metru and collecting souvenirs. Through a business in his home, he trades these souvenirs for other things he wants. Unfortunately, he often likes to make his trips during working hours, and the Vahki have to haul him back.

TA-METRU

THE FIRE PITS

These flame geysers are believed by the Matoran to be the source of all fire in Ta-Metru. Due to its importance, the entire area is fenced in and heavily guarded by Vahki patrols. Matoran must receive special permission from Turaga Dume to come here, because the unpredictable geysers are highly dangerous. The Ta-Metru Great Disk was hidden deep inside a fire pit.

PROTODERMIS RECLAMATION YARD

Ta-Matoran consider this to be a place best avoided. It is here that damaged masks and tools are sent to wait their turn in the furnaces, where they will be melted down. The resulting liquid protodermis will then be used to make other things. Mask makers consider the yard to be a monument to failure. Some say its caretaker has been on the job too long and talks to the empty masks as if they were living beings.

TOA VAKAMA

Element: Fire

Tool: Kanoka disk launcher

Mask: Kanohi Huna, the Great Mask of Concealment. Allows the user to turn invisible, although the user will still cast a shadow.

Vakama was a skilled Matoran mask maker before a crisis led to his transformation into a Toa. Despite the change, he remains unsure if he is cut out to be a hero. He has the potential to be a great leader, but only time will tell if he takes on the role.

One of the things that makes Vakama question his destiny is his strange ability to see into the future. He sees frightening visions that tell him of dangers ahead. It was one of these visions that inspired him to search for the Great Disks in order to save the city from the Morbuzakh. Some of the other Toa, particularly Onewa, think Vakama has spent too much time around open flames and that is why his head is "cross wired."

Vakama has shown great bravery and the ability to come up with daring plans. He blames himself for the disappearance of Toa Lhikan and is determined to find his hero and free him.

NUHRII

Nuhrii had been a mask maker for some time before Vakama was ever promoted to the position. It did not take long for Vakama's skills to surpass Nuhrii's, and soon he was getting all the special requests for masks from Turaga Dume. Nuhrii resented this and decided that he could outshine Vakama if he got the Ta-Metru Great Disk and made it into a Mask of Power. Nuhrii was lured into a trap by others who wanted the disk, and he was almost killed by Morbuzakh vines. Vakama saved his former coworker, and Nuhrii later helped the Toa find the Great Disk. Nuhrii disappeared shortly after the Toa defeated the Morbuzakh.

TA-METRU

NUURAKH

Swift and fearless, the Nuurakh protect Ta-Metru from wild Rahi and other threats. Some say they even behave like Rahi — they prefer to hunt from ambush, surrounding their target before he can react. But if they cannot find who they are searching for, they have been known to turn on each other. Other Vahki have even had to be called in to break up their fights! Nuurakh Staffs of Command fill the Matoran's mind with one overriding directive, which the affected being will then obey until the stun wears off hours later.

CREATURES OF TA-METRU

Lava Eels

These serpents thrive on heat, and love to be near molten protodermis pools. When they are little, they are often adopted by Ta-Matoran as pets, then abandoned when they get too large and destructive. When agitated, a lava eel's skin heats up and the creature can melt through solid rock.

Fireflyers

These flying insects have a fiery sting. Individually, they are harmless, but an angry swarm is capable of overcoming even a Toa Metru. They have been known to nest in furnaces and in the maintenance tunnels beneath the metru.

THE COLISEUM

The largest, most imposing structure in Metru Nui, the Coliseum is the center of power in the city in more ways than one. It sits at the meeting point of the six metru boundaries and is believed to have been the very first building constructed in Metru Nui. It can be seen from any point in the city and has always been a symbol to Matoran of stability and security.

The Coliseum has many features, including:

Sports arena: The Coliseum hosts the citywide Akilini tournaments, held four times a year. In this sport, up to six teams of a dozen players each compete to see who can hurl the most Kanoka disks through hoops arrayed along the top of the arena. To make it more challenging, the players all "surf" on disks over a constantly undulating floor as well as fly through retractable chutes positioned overhead. It's extremely fast-paced and dangerous. The winning team's disks are sent to Ta-Metru to be made into Kanohi masks.

The arena is also used for Vahki training exercises.

Main power source: The Coliseum houses the city's one power plant. Energy is generated by the flow of liquid protodermis through the plant on its way to other parts of the city. Although the plant does provide power for things like protodermis vat conveyors and chute controls, it does not provide heat to the city. This is done using pipes filled with molten protodermis that run underground and warm the buildings above.

Storage: Prior to the construction of the Great Temple, the Coliseum storage room was used to hold Kanohi Masks of Power. Since then, it has continued to be used to hold items of critical importance to the city. Security is provided by rotating squads of Vahki Rorzakh from Onu-Metru and Vahki Zadakh from Po-Metru.

Turaga Dume's box: This special section is reserved for the Turaga and commands a view of the entire arena. From here, Dume can control the massive telescreens that are mounted all over the city as well as in the Coliseum. The box is equipped with levitation and increase weight Kanoka disks that allow it to be raised and lowered at the Turaga's will.

Turaga Dume's throne room: This chamber is connected to Dume's box in the arena. In the past, it has been used for private meetings with the Turaga on issues of importance to the city. But in recent months Dume has been far too busy for such appointments and no one has been allowed to visit his private chamber, other than Vahki guards.

CITY OF METRU NUI

THE COLISEUM

TURAGA DUME

Element: **Fire**

Mask: **Kanohi Kiril, Great Mask of Regeneration**

Turaga Dume has been a wise and just elder of Metru Nui for as long as any Matoran can remember. Under his leadership, the chute system was constructed, the Vahki order enforcement squads were created, and the Archives were expanded to their present size. He is admired and respected by Matoran everywhere.

Recently, Dume has begun hinting that some great disaster is heading for Metru Nui. While he will not explain its nature, it has worried him enough that he went to Vakama to ask for the creation of a Great Mask of Time. How he plans to use this mask is unknown.

TOA LHIKAN

Element: **Fire**

Mask: **Kanohi Hau, the Great Mask of Shielding**

Tool: Lhikan carries two fire greatswords, which can be merged together to form a fire board. Lhikan can ride it like a surfboard, and it is capable of flight. He can often be seen soaring high above the city.

Little is known about Toa Lhikan's past. It is said he came to Metru Nui from some other place, for reasons that he declines to discuss. He has served as the lone protector of the city for many, many years, and Matoran in every metru look up to him. With few threats to Metru Nui,

Lhikan has largely kept busy helping the Vahki to capture particularly dangerous Rahi.

After the Morbuzakh began attacking the city, Lhikan became suspicious that there was more going on than might at first appear. His doubts increased when he discovered that two Dark Hunters, Nidhiki and Krekka, were searching for him. Knowing he could not elude them for long, Lhikan transferred some of his Toa power into six Toa stones and gave them to Matoran from different metru. Shortly after that, Lhikan was kidnapped by the Dark Hunters and has not been seen since. His fate remains unknown.

THE DARK HUNTERS

Although no Dark Hunters had ever been spotted before in Metru Nui, whispers of their existence had reached the ears of Matoran from other places. The Dark Hunters are said to be as powerful as Toa, but they are far from being heroes. They will take any job, no matter how evil or destructive, if the reward is great enough. The presence of Dark Hunters in the city is a sign of much greater danger to come.

NIDHIKI

Affiliation: Dark Hunters

Abilities: Can spit energy bolts; can launch Kanoka disks.

This multi-legged monster first appeared in Metru Nui shortly after the Morbuzakh began menacing Matoran. Nidhiki and his brutish partner, Krekka, kidnapped Toa Lhikan and attempted to stop the Toa Metru from finding the six Great Disks.

Nidhiki is vicious and cunning, with no regard for duty or honor. He is

Nidhiki is vicious and cunning, with no regard for duty or honor. He is extremely intelligent and understands that fear can sometimes be a more powerful tool than force. From things Toa Lhikan said to him, it would appear the two must have known each other sometime in the past.

KREKKA

Affiliation: Dark Hunters

Abilities: Can generate and project energy webs; can launch Kanoka disks.

What Krekka lacks in brains, he more than makes up for in brute strength. Most of the time, just his presence is enough to frighten someone into doing whatever Nidhiki wants. His destructive ways can make him seem like a wild Rahi in a Knowledge Tower at times.

Krekka is most effective when he is following one of Nidhiki's plans. When he tries something on his own, he usually causes lots of damage without really accomplishing much. But when you are as powerful as Krekka, it is easy to fight your way out of any trap you may have walked into.

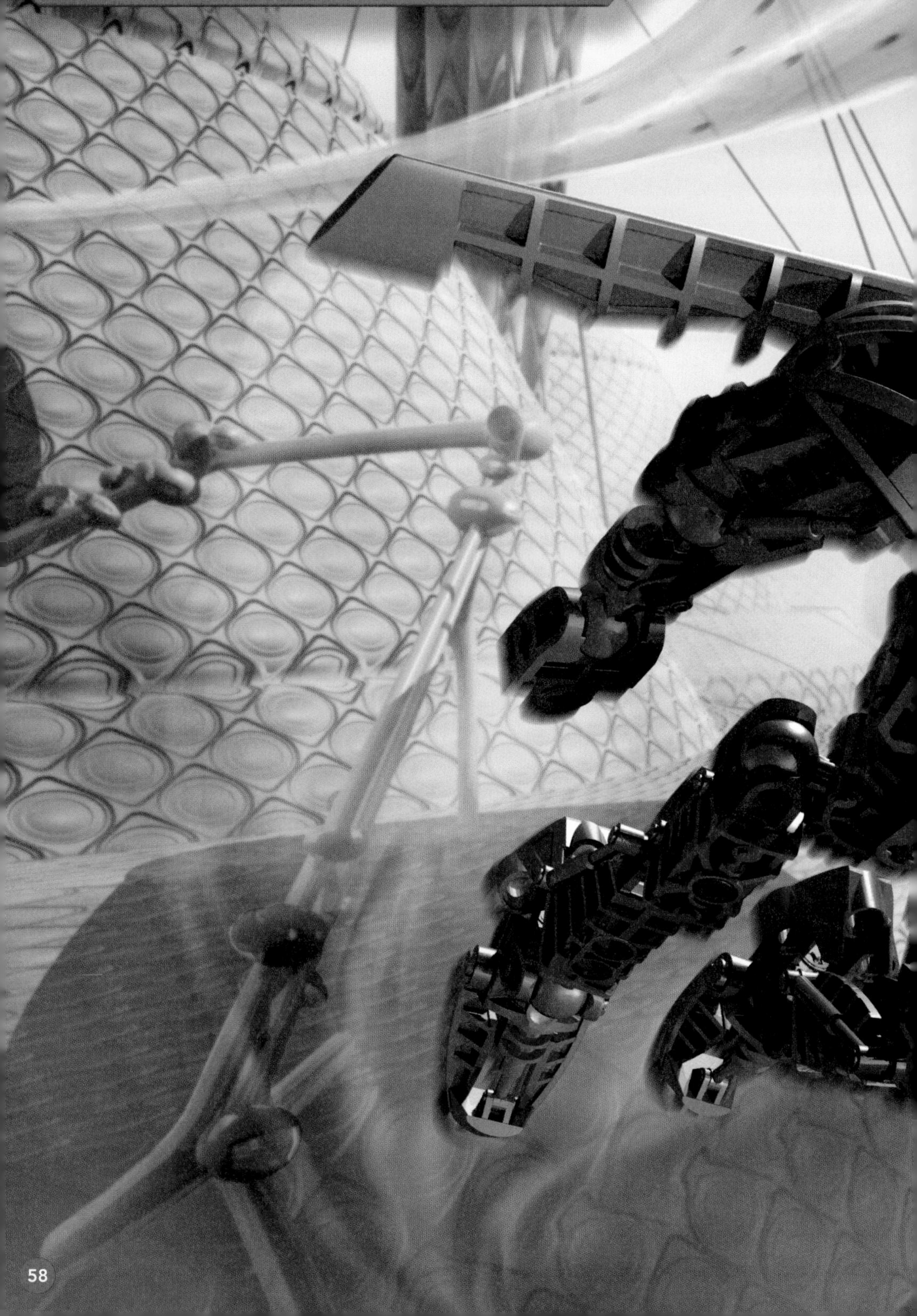

Walking into Le-Metru is like walking into a dense jungle. The ground is littered with tools and wires that can snag your feet. Covering much of the metru is a canopy of tangled cables and chutes that, in some places, almost block out the suns. The air is filled with the constant chatter of Le-Matoran hard at work among the chutes. The feeling is one of barely contained chaos.

The Le-Matoran are allowed to have a metru that is something of a mess because their work is so vital to the city as a whole. Le-Metru is the transport center for Metru Nui. Here chutes and vehicles are built and maintained to insure the smooth flow of Matoran and cargo from one place to another. Without the efforts of Le-Matoran, the tools forged in Ta-Metru could never get to Po-Metru for finishing and the Rahi captured in Ga-Metru would never make it to the Archives. In short, Metru Nui would grind to a halt.

All of this has combined to make the Le-Matoran very brash and confident. They know how important they are. They like to make sure that everyone else knows it, too.

THE MOTO-HUB

The center of Le-Metru is the Moto-Hub, home to the vehicle manufacturing factories and the chute system controls. Roughly half of the Le-Matoran work here. The rest mainly do repair and maintenance work in Le-Metru or elsewhere in the city.

Le-Matoran work on three major types of transport: chutes, air vehicles, and ground vehicles. They refuse to make boats, because Le-Matoran hate the sea, so any watercraft is created in Ga-Metru.

Here is a quick look at the ways to get around Metru Nui:

Chutes: The primary transport system for the city. Chutes are long cylindrical tubes made of liquid protodermis held in place by a sheath of magnetic energy. Magnetized protodermis flows through the chutes at high speed, carrying with it Matoran and cargo on their way to and from different metru. Most chutes run aboveground, in some cases high above, held aloft by a system of solid protodermis braces. Some run below the surface to reach different levels of the Archives, but many of the subterranean chutes are in bad repair and too dangerous to use. Few Le-Matoran want to go down below to fix them.

Chutes run at varying speeds, although the preferred rates in Le-Metru are fast, very fast, and way too fast. Every chute runs in a preset direction. Reversing the flow of a chute, and thus changing its direction, is considered to be highly dangerous. The main chute controls are the responsibility of a Matoran named Kongu.

There are two ways to board a chute. The recommended way is at a chute station. These stations are located all over Metru Nui. Here the flow of the chute slows down enough that boarding can be done safely and easily.

The other method, "chute jumping," is illegal although still done by some of the more daring Matoran. Chute jumping involves leaping onto a chute during the split seconds that the magnetic energy wavers so

that you pass through the outer layer of force and into the chute itself. There are two reasons this is risky: First, if the jump is not timed right, the jumper can smack into the outer layer hard and possibly fall off the chute and plunge to the ground. Second, jumping into a high-speed chute increases the chances of being struck by another passenger or piece of cargo.

Some Matoran also do "disking" tricks in chutes. This involves riding through the chute while standing on top of a Kanoka disk, often doing flips or sliding along the walls or ceiling of the chute. This is very common in Le-Metru but is also a good way to catch the eyes of the Vahki.

Chutes face a number of problems. Sometimes portions physically break off, sending riders flying into space. In very old chutes, the braces may be in bad repair and the chute comes crashing to the ground, or else the magnetic energy sheath weakens and the liquid protodermis leaks out.

If a flaw develops in the chute's construction, a portion of the magnetic energy can break off and fold in on itself, becoming a force sphere. It then flies through the chute, its intense pull drawing in tools, cargo, debris, and anything else floating in the chute. As it does so, the sphere gets bigger and bigger. Eventually, it tears the chute to pieces and then implodes.

Air vehicles: Air transport is used only for cargo in Metru Nui. Huge vessels float through the skies, carrying Rahi to Onu-Metru, solid protodermis blocks and tools to Po-Metru, and other bulk items to points around the city. Matoran airships work thanks to a complicated system of Kanoka levitation disks and increase weight disks. When the pulleys cause the levitation disks to strike the framework, the craft rises. For landing, a different set of pulleys causes the increase weight disks to strike and the ship goes down. It can take years for a Le-Matoran to master the system and so pilots are highly respected.

Ground vehicles: The two major types of land vehicle in Metru Nui are Ussal carts and Vahki transports. Ussal carts are wagons pulled by tame Rahi called Ussal crabs. Although they sometimes carry passengers, these carts are normally used to transport cargo.

Vahki transports are much larger vehicles, which are used to ferry large numbers of Vahki from one place to another. Kanoka disks of speed are built into the structure so that the transport can move swiftly. Motive power is provided by insectoid like legs on both sides of the vehicle. Le-Matoran have been experimenting with the notion of replacing disk power with energy given off by living creatures, but they have not succeeded in making this work.

LE-METRU

TEST TRACK

Matoran are always trying to develop new types of vehicles that will be faster and more efficient. All of them need to be tested before they can be put into use, so they are brought to the Le-Metru test track. When he was a Matoran, Matau was a frequent visitor to the track and loved to take new vehicles out and see what they could do. He didn't even mind all the spinouts, crashes, and explosions that went with the job!

DON'T MISS ...

Tamaru's Transports

This fast-talking Matoran rents and sells used Ussal carts, failed test track vehicles, and other modes of transport from his shop. After washing out as an airship pilot because of his fear of heights, Tamaru decided it made more sense to have a career firmly on the ground. For Matoran who want a change from riding in chutes, this is the place to go.

TOA MATAU

Element: Air

Tools: Twin aero slicers, that can act as glider wings

Mask: Kanohi Mahiki, the Great Mask of Illusion. Allows Matau to shapeshift and take on the appearance and voice of anyone he chooses.

Of all the Matoran turned Toa Metru, it is Matau who is happiest about the change. Even when he was just an Ussal cart driver, he dreamed of being a famous hero. Now that it has happened, he intends to enjoy every minute of it. Deep inside, he worries that he may not be able to live up to his own image of what a Toa should be. As a result, he sometimes shows off or takes needless chances to prove to others that he is truly a "Toa-hero." He particularly wants to impress Nokama, but she has shown no sign of interest in the impulsive Toa Metru of Air.

ORKAHM

Orkahm is a chief Ussal cart driver in Le-Metru. Slow and methodical by nature, he has always envied Matau's speed and quick wit. When he spotted a Great Disk, he thought the discovery would make him famous. Instead, he was kidnapped by Nidhiki and had to be rescued by Toa Matau. After that, he decided maybe fame wasn't worth the risk. Orkahm disappeared after the defeat of the Morbuzakh and has not been seen since.

VORZAKH

Unlike most Vahki, the Vorzakh don't really seem to enjoy chasing lawbreakers. If they need to find someone, they simply level everything in their path until they locate him. Vorzakh Staffs of Erasing are incredibly powerful, able to temporarily eliminate higher mental functions in Matoran, leaving only motor functions intact. Le-Matoran have grown used to seeing these unfortunates, called "shamblers," wandering through the metru.

CREATURES OF LE-METRU

Kinloka

A particularly vicious form of large rodent, the Kinloka was the result of an experiment to produce a Rahi with a more efficient digestive system. The outcome was a creature that is constantly hungry and eats anything in its path. Although they have made a home in Le-Metru, the creatures have been seen all over the city. A swarm of Kinloka was once spotted consuming an entire Po-Metru assemblers' village — houses, tools, everything — all in less than fifteen minutes.

Gukko

These large birds roost in the tangle of cables above Le-Metru. Matau once made an attempt to ride one, which ended in dismal failure. He has since firmly stated that no one will ever be able to tame a Gukko bird.

ONU-METRU

Of all the residents of Metru Nui, Onu-Matoran are regarded as the most unusual. Whether they are mining lightstones or working deep in the Archives, they spend much of their lives underground. Other metru citizens cannot understand how they manage to exist like this, but to Onu-Matoran it seems the most natural thing in the world.

Most Onu-Matoran work in the Archives, but they do not see it as a job. They love helping to preserve the history of Metru Nui and will brave any danger to protect the institution. It is very rare that a Vahki has to force an Onu-Matoran to go back to work — given the choice, some would never leave their exhibit halls.

ONU-METRU

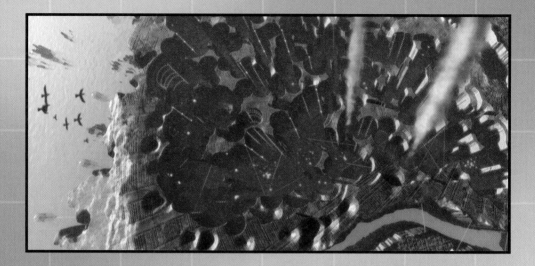

THE GREAT ARCHIVES

The Archives is the largest single institution in all of Metru Nui. It encompasses most of the surface of Onu-Metru and extends underground for multiple levels. After years of expansion the Archives now stretches beneath almost all of the city.

This massive museum is filled with artifacts and specimens of every Rahi ever found within the city limits. What the Knowledge Towers are to prophecies and written records, the Archives is to everything else. Tools, Kanohi masks, disks, art objects, and strange and bizarre creatures take up all the available space in this building.

The upper levels of the Archives are open to the public and frequently visited by groups of students from Ga-Metru. The lower levels are restricted and are the site of research and experiments.

By far the most popular attractions in the Archives are the various Rahi on display. These creatures are captured by Vahki and brought to Onu-Metru, where crews of Matoran put them into stasis tubes. These consist of two separate casings, inner and outer. Once inside, a variation on Kraahu stun gas is used to throw the Rahi into suspended animation.

This is not a perfect system. To keep the Rahi from perishing, the gas used must be very weak. This means if the inner casing should become cracked, enough air will leak in to awaken the Rahi. More often than not, it will then break free and go on a destructive rampage until it is finally subdued by Vahki Rorzakh. For this reason, great care is taken to make sure Rahi tubes are not damaged in transport.

The nature of the gas also makes it difficult to hold extremely large creatures in stasis. These are kept in cages or cells in the sublevels, along with creatures deemed too dangerous to have anywhere near the public levels, regardless of whether they are awake or not. Many Onu-Matoran do their best to avoid being assigned to work on these lower levels.

Beneath the lower levels is a network of maintenance tunnels. These tunnels are so dark and confusing that the Onu-Matoran have nicknamed them the "Fikou web," after the tangled strands woven by the Fikou spider.

Here are only a few of the creatures now held in the Archives:

Rahkshi: These armored monsters have appeared at various times and in various points of the city. A small number have been captured by the Vahki, but many more escaped and may be hiding beneath the city.

Bohrok: Onu-Matoran miners stumbled upon what seemed to be a nest of insectlike creatures some time ago. They are now on display in the public levels, while the organic creatures called *krana* who were also found in the nest are held in the lower levels.

Two-headed Tarakava and Mutant Ussal Crab: Once in a while Matoran encounter strange mutations of known Rahi. A biheaded sea beast was captured by Bordakh in the last six months. It has resisted stasis and is being held in a water tank on a sublevel. Nearby is an incredibly huge version of the common Ussal crab, which was possibly crossbred with some other monstrous Rahi. It, too, has resisted stasis and is kept locked up.

Unknowns: Many of the creatures in the lower levels of the Archives have never been identified by the Onu-Matoran. These include a Rahi that seems to be made completely of smoke; another that can look like virtually anything, including its cell; a large insectoid that can

DON'T MISS...

Nuparu's Workshop

Nuparu is an inventive, brilliant Matoran who is always putting things together and taking them apart. He came up with the design for the Vahki, helped create the Le-Metru airships, and has made many other contributions to daily life. His next big project is to come up with some kind of device or vehicle that would help Matoran defend themselves against Rahi and other threats.

create a thick crystalline nest for itself in a matter of moments; and microscopic protodites, that escaped their containment cell long ago and have been loose in the Archives ever since.

Also included in this category are a large number of sea beasts held in the Archives for study some years ago. Due to the danger they presented to the city, Turaga Dume took the unusual step of ordering that they be driven from Metru Nui and prevented from returning. The creatures escaped captivity before this could happen and have not been seen anywhere around the city since.

PRISON OF THE DARK HUNTERS

This subterranean site is being used by the Dark Hunters to hold their captives. No one knows who may be in there or why the Dark Hunters are taking prisoners at all. It is expected that the Vahki will handle this situation in time.

TOA WHENUA

Element: Earth

Mask: Kanohi Ruru, the Great Mask of Night Vision

Tools: Twin earthshock drills

Toa Whenua is not as bold and confident as some of the other Toa Metru. Being a former archivist, he knows all the stories about disasters that befell Matoran who rushed into things without thinking. He believes caution, planning, and a knowledge of the past are the most important tools for a hero. Unless, of course, the exhibits in the Archives are threatened — then he takes risks of every kind to protect what he views as the most important place in all of Metru Nui.

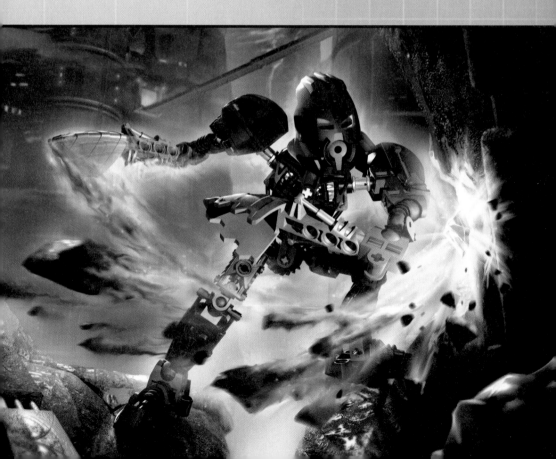

TEHUTTI

Tehutti has spent virtually all of his life working in the Onu-Metru Archives. He is a sensible, practical, hardworking Matoran but has never received the recognition he felt was his due. When he found a Great Disk in the Archives, he became convinced such an enormous discovery would make him famous. Instead, it got him trapped by Dark Hunters and almost killed by Rahkshi. He later agreed to help Whenua find the disk. His current whereabouts are unknown.

RORZAKH

Vahki Rorzakh have the important job of protecting the Archives. They are the most relentless of all Vahki, never giving up on a chase. Rorzakh Staffs of Presence have the longest-lasting effects, allowing the Vahki to see and hear whatever the affected Matoran does without the Matoran being aware of it.

CREATURES OF ONU-METRU

Krahka

This female Rahi lurks in the maintenance tunnels beneath the Archives sublevels. She has the ability to take on the appearance, characteristics, and powers of anything she encounters. When the Toa entered the tunnels, she attempted to use her talents to make them destroy each other. When that failed, she planned to lure the population of Metru Nui into the tunnels, seal them up, and rule the city herself. The Toa Metru stopped her, but the Krahka escaped. Her whereabouts are currently unknown.

Kraawa

This Rahi may not seem particularly dangerous, but it is kept in the most highly secured portion of the Archives. Its defense against predators is to absorb any force directed against it and use that energy to grow. The specimen currently in stasis grew to half the size of a Knowledge Tower and wrecked three levels of the Archives before it was subdued. Whether others of its kind exist somewhere remains a mystery.

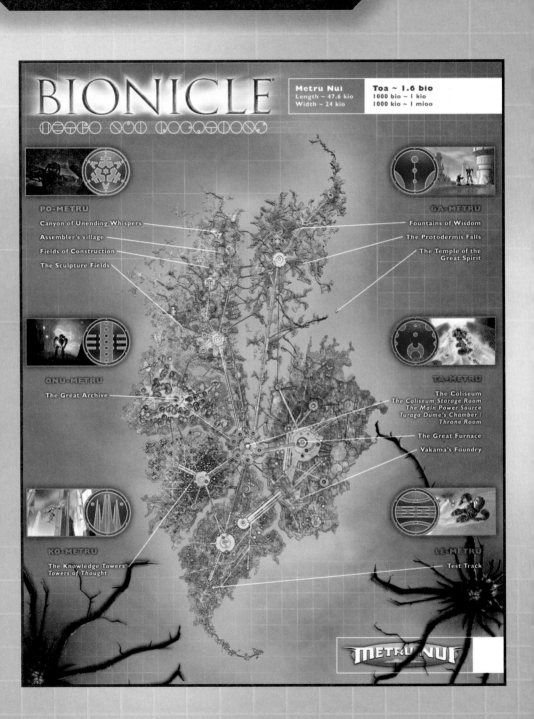

BIONICLE

ᒷᑎᖶᑌ ᑎᑌᓰ ᒪᓍᑕᐋᖶᓰᓍᑎᔑ

Metru Nui	Toa ~ 1.6 bio
Length ~ 47.6 kio	1000 bio ~ 1 kio
Width ~ 24 kio	1000 kio ~ 1 mioo

PO-METRU
Canyon of Unending Whispers
Assembler's village
Fields of Construction
The Sculpture Fields

GA-METRU
Fountains of Wisdom
The Protodermis Falls
The Temple of the Great Spirit

ONU-METRU
The Great Archive

TA-METRU
The Coliseum
The Coliseum Storage Room
The Main Power Source
Turaga Dume's Chamber /
Throne Room
The Great Furnace
Vakama's Foundry

KO-METRU
The Knowledge Towers
Towers of Thought

LE-METRU
Test Track

METRU NUI

THE SAGA CONTINUES
IN A CITY OF LEGENDS

The six Toa Metru face a dark and dangerous conspiracy in the heart of Metru Nui — one that threatens their friends, their home, and even their very existence as Toa. Before all is done, they will have to challenge the greatest powers of their city, survive shocking betrayal, and see a Toa fall, never to rise again.

To learn more about Metru Nui, go to www.metrunui.com and enter the ISBN from the copyright page of this book. Then enter this special code:

246

BIONICLE

FIND THE POWER, LIVE THE LEGEND

The legend comes alive in these exciting BIONICLE™ books:

BIONICLE™ Chronicles
#1 Tale of the Toa
#2 Beware the Bohrok
#3 Makuta's Revenge
#4 Tales of the Masks

The Official Guide to BIONICLE™

BIONICLE™ Collector's Sticker Book

BIONICLE™: Mask of Light

BIONICLE™ Adventures
#1 Mystery of Metru Nui
#2 Trial by Fire
#3 The Darkness Below